NEPTUNE

GOD OF THE SEA AND EARTHQUAKES

by Teri Temple and Emily Temple
Illustrated by Eric Young

Published by The Child's World®
1980 Lookout Drive • Mankato, MN 56003-1705
800-599-READ • www.childsworld.com

ACKNOWLEDGMENTS
The Child's World®: Mary Berendes, Publishing Director
Red Line Editorial: Editorial direction
The Design Lab: Design and production
Design elements ©: Banana Republic Images/Shutterstock Images; Shutterstock Images;
Anton Balazh/Shutterstock Images
Photographs ©: Viacheslav Lopatin/Shutterstock Images, 5; Hollygraphic/Shutterstock
Images, 13; Remy Musser/Shutterstock Images, 16; Yuriy Kulik/Shutterstock Images,
21; Malgorzata Kistryn/Shutterstock Images, 24; NASA, 29

ISBN 9781631437229
LCCN 2014945314

Printed in the United States of America
Mankato, MN
November, 2014
PA02241

TABLE *of* CONTENTS

INTRODUCTION

In ancient times Romans believed in spirits or gods called numina. In Latin, *numina* means divine will or power. The Romans took part in religious rituals to please the gods. They felt the gods had powers that could make their lives better.

As the Roman government grew more powerful, its armies conquered many neighboring lands. Romans often adopted beliefs from these new cultures. They greatly admired the Greek arts and sciences. Gradually, the Romans combined the Greek myths and religion with their own. These stories shaped and influenced each part of a Roman citizen's daily life. Ancient Roman poets, such as Ovid and Virgil, wrote down these tales of wonder. Their writings became a part of Rome's great history. To the Romans, however, these stories were not just for entertainment. Roman mythology was their key to understanding the world.

ANCIENT ROMAN SOCIETIES
Ancient Roman society was divided into several groups. The patricians were the most powerful and wealthiest group. They often owned land and held power in the government. The plebeians worked for the patricians. Slaves were prisoners of war or children without parents. Some slaves were freed and enjoyed most of the rights of citizens.

ANCIENT ROME

N

W

S

ADRIATIC SEA

ROME

TYRRHENIAN SEA

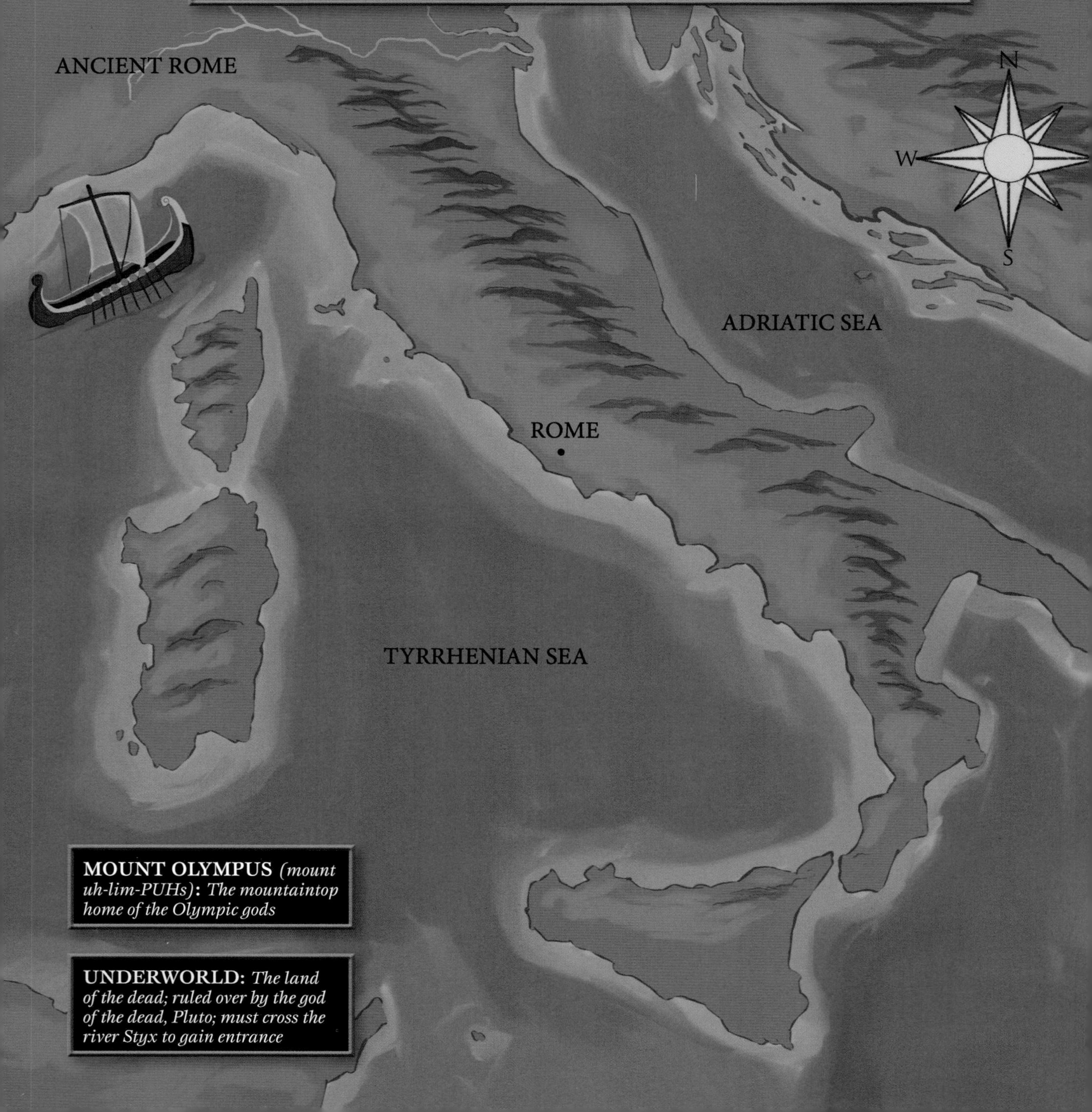

MOUNT OLYMPUS *(mount uh-lim-PUHs)*: *The mountaintop home of the Olympic gods*

UNDERWORLD: *The land of the dead; ruled over by the god of the dead, Pluto; must cross the river Styx to gain entrance*

JUPITER *(JOO-pi-ter)*

Supreme ruler of the heavens and of the gods on Mount Olympus; son of Saturn and Ops; married to Juno; father of many gods and heroes

MARS *(mahrz)*

God of war; son of Jupiter and Juno; possible father of Cupid

NEPTUNE *(NEP-toon)*

God of the seas and earthquakes; brother to Jupiter

OTUS AND EPHIALTES *(OH-tuhs and Eff-ee-ALL-tees)*

Enormous twin giants; sons of Neptune

PEGASUS *(PEG-uh-suhs)*

A winged horse that sprang from the neck of the beheaded Medusa

PLUTO *(PLOO-toh)*

God of the underworld and death; son of Saturn and Ops; married to Proserpine.

POLYPHEMUS *(pah-luh-FEE-muhs)*

Man-eating giant blinded by Odysseus; son of Neptune

SALACIA *(suh-LEY-shuh)*

Sea nymph, goddess of the sea; wife of Neptune

SATURN *(SAT-ern)*

A Titan who ruled the world; married to Ops, their children became the first six Olympic gods

GOD OF THE SEA

Neptune was the god of the sea. He ruled over all the oceans and seas. He was a very powerful god. And he was as unpredictable as the storms he created. However, his story begins with his powerful father, Saturn, and brother Jupiter.

Saturn was a very mighty god. He was married to Ops. Together, they had six children: Vesta, Neptune, Pluto, Ceres, Juno, and Jupiter. Even though Saturn was the most powerful being in the universe, he was afraid of losing his power. A prophecy had told him one of his children would overthrow him. To prevent this from happening, Saturn swallowed each of his children right after they were born.

Ops hatched a plan to stop her husband. When her sixth child, Jupiter, was born, she took Jupiter far away. Jupiter grew into a strong and powerful god. He knew he had to free his siblings from their father. Together with his grandmother, Terra, he gave Saturn a special potion to drink. Saturn threw up his children, freeing them.

Neptune and his siblings were finally free. All the gods were unharmed. But they were angry. They went to war against Saturn to gain control of the universe. Along with an army of Cyclopes and Hecatoncheires, Neptune and his siblings fought hard.

The Cyclopes made weapons to help them in war. One of these weapons was Neptune's mighty trident. It was a three-pronged spear that could shake the universe. With it, Neptune was able to show his great strength. The Cyclopes also created Jupiter's thunderbolts and an invisibility helmet for Pluto. With their weapons, the three brothers worked together to defeat Saturn.

After the gods' victory over Saturn, peace settled over the land. But they needed to agree on a new supreme leader. Neptune hoped it would be him. Neptune, Pluto, and Jupiter decided to draw lots. Jupiter was the lucky one. He drew the best lot. As a result, he became the new king of the gods. Jupiter divided the universe between himself and his brothers. Neptune was made the god of the seas. Pluto was to rule the underworld.

Neptune was a powerful ruler of the seas. He was also the god of horses and earthquakes. The Greek poet Homer called him the "Earth shaker." Neptune is often depicted as a giant with a beard and wavy black hair. Neptune always carried his special trident.

This three-pronged weapon gave Neptune control over the seas and oceans of the world. Using his trident, he could divide, stir, or calm the waters. Neptune had the power to raise or quiet mighty storms. He traveled across the water in a seashell chariot drawn by four green seahorses that were covered in scales. The horses had golden manes and brass hooves. Dolphins often jumped at Neptune's side as he rode along with his horses.

Unfortunately, Neptune had a bit of a temper. If someone made Neptune mad, he would send a raging storm or flood. He often fought back without a second thought. Because of his bad temper and powers, ancient Romans blamed Neptune for all shipwrecks and drownings. Neptune's attendants were the Tritons, the Nereids, and the Dioscuri. The Tritons and the Dioscuri helped Neptune shipwreck sailors. The Nereids were female sea nymphs. They were often friendly to those at sea.

THE DIOSCURI

The Dioscuri were twins. They were also called Castor and Pollux. They helped Neptune shipwreck sailors. According to the Roman legends, Castor was a mortal. But Pollux was the son of Jupiter, which meant he was a god. When Castor was murdered, Jupiter gave Pollux a choice. Pollux could spend all of his time on Mount Olympus, or he could give half of his immortality to his mortal brother. If he chose the second option, they could alternate realms together. Pollux decided to share his immortality. In some myths, they became the constellation Gemini.

One mortal to face Neptune's wrath was Andromeda. She was the princess of Ethiopia. Her mother was Cassiopeia. Cassiopeia bragged that Andromeda was more beautiful than the water nymphs of the sea. As the god of the sea, Neptune was insulted. He planned to get revenge by sending a sea monster to attack the coast of Ethiopia.

Cassiopeia discovered that the only way to appease Neptune was to sacrifice Andromeda. So she had her daughter chained to the cliffs of Ethiopia. She hoped it would save her country. Luckily for her, a hero named Perseus killed the sea monster and saved Andromeda. Surprisingly, Neptune did not punish Perseus for killing his sea monster. This may be because Perseus was well liked by the gods. Perseus even used Pluto's invisibility helmet. Jupiter's children Minerva and Mercury also helped Perseus save Andromeda. Minerva lent Perseus her shield, and Mercury lent his winged sandals.

Neptune fell in love with a beautiful sea nymph. Her name was Salacia. Ancient Romans compared her to the Greek goddess Amphitrite, queen of the sea. Salacia was gentle and shy. She was in awe of Neptune, so she hid from him in the Atlantic Ocean.

Neptune sent a dolphin out to sea to find Salacia. The dolphin convinced her to return and marry Neptune. When he heard the news, Neptune was so happy he gave the dolphin a place in heaven amongst the stars.

After they were married, Salacia often rode with Neptune in his chariot, wearing a crown of seaweed. They lived together in a marvelous palace, deep on the ocean floor. It was covered in gold and adorned with coral and gems.

PAREDRAE

The original Roman water god was Neptunus. Instead of having a wife, Neptunus had two paredrae, or water deities. In Roman religion, they were most often female. Neptunus's paredrae were named Salacia and Venilia. They represented flooding waters and still waters. By the first century BC, Neptune took over the role as Roman god of the sea.

Neptune and Salacia had many children together. Three of their daughters were sea nymphs. They would go on to marry a king, a giant, and a god. The most famous of their children was their son, Triton. He was half man and half fish. He served as Neptune's messenger. Like his father, Triton had godlike powers. He could also calm the sea. Salacia is also credited as being the mother of seals, dolphins, fish, and shellfish.

Neptune loved Salacia. But he was not always faithful to her. He had many other wives and children. Some of Neptune's wives were mortal. He had many mortal children with these wives. Three of these children were Orion and twins named Otus and Ephialtes. All three were giants. Otus and Ephialtes thought they were better than the gods. They challenged the gods to prove their power. Once, Otus and Ephialtes kidnapped Mars, the god of war. They held Mars hostage. Mars was only set free when Mercury, the god of travel, freed him.

Neptune often had to save his children from the trouble they caused. One time, the twins tried to stack up mountains to reach Mount Olympus. They picked up one mountain and placed it on another. Just as Jupiter was about to strike them down with his thunderbolts for their foolishness, Neptune urged Jupiter to spare them.

Even with his powers, Neptune was not always able to save his twins. One day, the twins tried to capture the goddesses Diana and Juno. Diana ran away, so Otus and Ephialtes chased her. But eventually she disappeared. In her place, the twins saw a beautiful white stag. They threw spears at it, but the animal disappeared. The spears flew at the twins instead. Both twins were killed.

ORION
Neptune's son Orion fell in love with the goddess Diana. When they met, Diana and Orion quickly became friends. They often hunted together. According to one legend, Diana accidentally killed Orion during one of their hunting trips. She was very sad. As a form of respect, she decided to place him in the stars. The constellation Orion is easily identifiable by a row of three stars that make up his belt.

Neptune had another son he had to help save. This son was Polyphemus. He was a monstrous, man-eating Cyclops. Polyphemus lived alone on an island. His job was to tend a flock of sheep.

The hero Odysseus traveled to Polyphemus's island on his way home from war. On the island, Odysseus and his men discovered a cave filled with food. It was the home of Polyphemus. When Polyphemus discovered the men snooping around inside, he decided to trap them. He blocked the entrance with a boulder and planned to eat them in the morning.

Little did Polyphemus know, Odysseus was clever. When Polyphemus arrived back at the cave that evening, Odysseus gave him wine. Polyphemus drank too much and fell asleep. While he was sleeping, Odysseus shoved a stake into his only eye.

Polyphemus was furious. He needed to let his sheep out, but he feared the men would take advantage of his blindness and escape. He blocked the door with his giant body and felt each sheep as it passed. Odysseus and his men hid themselves underneath the bellies of the sheep and escaped. Polyphemus begged Neptune for help. He asked Neptune to prevent Odysseus from ever making it home. Neptune agreed. He caused problems at sea and made Odysseus's trip last 10 long years.

Ancient Greeks and Romans believed Neptune was responsible for creating the horse. He was inspired to do so because he wanted to impress a woman. Neptune had fallen madly in love with Ceres. She was the goddess of grain and the harvest.

One day, Ceres presented a challenge to Neptune. She asked him to create the most beautiful animal the world had ever seen. Neptune worked for many days to make the animal perfect. Finally, he produced a gorgeous horse. When she saw it, Ceres was amazed and

CERES
Demeter was the Greek counterpart to the Roman goddess Ceres. Her job was to reign over the harvest. If Ceres was ever upset, ancient Romans believed that the crops would die. As a result, both gods and mortals worked hard to keep Ceres happy.

impressed. Neptune was overjoyed and created a whole herd of horses for her. For himself, he made green horses to fill the stables at his golden palace in the sea. These green horses pulled Neptune in his chariot across the surface of the water. They had brass hooves and golden manes.

However, legend has it that Neptune made a few mistakes before he came up with the horse. Ancient people believe that the giraffe, the zebra, the hippopotamus, and the camel were all created by Neptune but cast aside as accidents. For his invention of the horse, Neptune was made the patron god of horse racing.

Neptune was a very restless god. He rarely stayed at his palace under the sea. Most often, Neptune could be found racing across the surface of the water in his seashell chariot. He loved all the creatures of the sea, but his favorite was his green horses. Many sea creatures were also his children. One impressive child was a giant sea monster named Charybdis. Charybdis was chained to the bottom of the sea because she created enormous whirlpools that endangered seafarers.

Neptune had a brief love affair with Medusa. Medusa was an attendant of the goddess Minerva. When Minerva found out about the affair, she transformed Medusa into a hideous monster. She gave Medusa writhing snakes instead of hair and the ability to turn men into stone just by making eye contact. Medusa was later beheaded. Pegasus sprung from her severed neck. Pegasus was the offspring of Neptune's affair. He was a wild and beautiful horse with wings. He would play a role in many of Neptune's stories.

The Roman god Neptune was based on the Greek god
of the sea, Poseidon. The Greeks were a seafaring people.
Poseidon was very important to them. In many ancient
cultures, a god of the sea was part of their pantheon of gods.
A pantheon is the collection of gods that a society worships.
Romans added Neptune to their pantheon.

Originally, Neptune was in charge of fresh waters. Ancient Romans reinforced this idea when they celebrated a festival in his honor each year. This festival was called Neptunalia. It was held in July as part of a series of festivals that honored the rain that ended the droughts of summer. In time, the sea and ocean waters were also put under Neptune's charge. Neptune would eventually rule over earthquakes and horses as well.

Neptune was known for his wide range of moods. His personality reflected the water he controlled. He was sometimes angry and tumultuous. Other times he was calm. Neptune had great strength and powers that struck fear in the hearts of his enemies, making him one of the greatest gods in ancient mythology.

THE PLANET NEPTUNE
Astronomers discovered the planet Neptune in 1846. Neptune is a blue planet surrounded by thin white clouds on its surface. The blue color reminded early astronomers of Earth's oceans and seas, so they named it Neptune after the god of the sea. Coincidentally, the climate on Neptune also reflects Neptune the god. The planet is very windy, with stronger winds than any other planet.

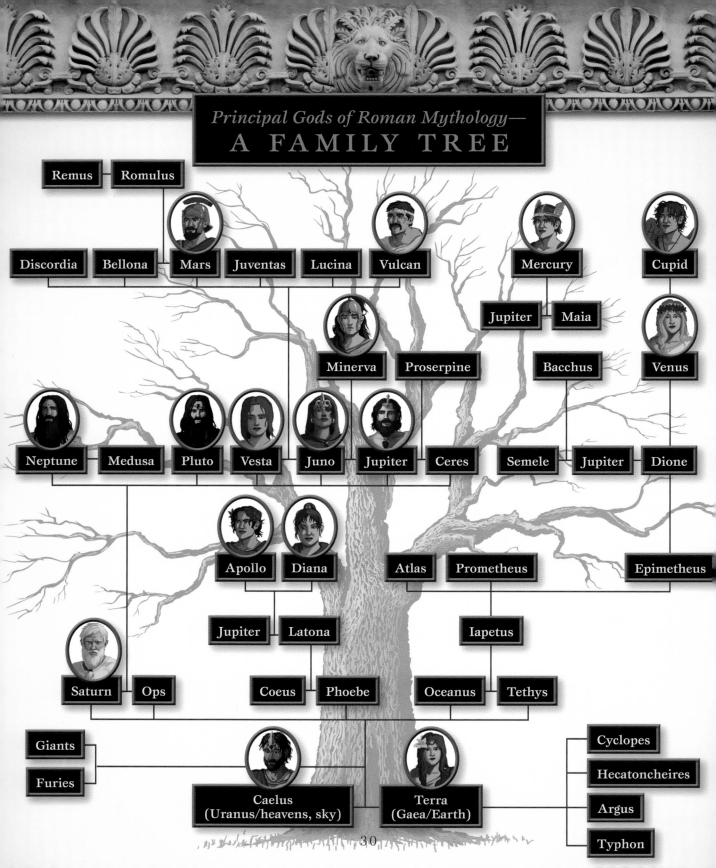

Principal Gods of Roman Mythology—
A FAMILY TREE

Remus — Romulus

Discordia — Bellona — Mars — Juventas — Lucina — Vulcan

Mercury

Cupid

Jupiter — Maia

Minerva — Proserpine

Bacchus

Venus

Neptune — Medusa — Pluto — Vesta — Juno — Jupiter — Ceres — Semele — Jupiter — Dione

Apollo — Diana — Atlas — Prometheus — Epimetheus

Jupiter — Latona — Iapetus

Coeus — Phoebe — Oceanus — Tethys

Saturn — Ops

Giants
Furies

Caelus
(Uranus/heavens, sky)

Terra
(Gaea/Earth)

Cyclopes
Hecatoncheires
Argus
Typhon

THE GREEK GODS

Ancient Greeks believed gods and goddesses ruled the world. The gods fell in love and struggled for power, but they never died. The ancient Greeks believed their gods were immortal. The Greek people worshiped the gods in temples. They felt the gods would protect and guide them. Over time, the Romans and many other cultures adopted the Greek myths as their own. While these other cultures changed the names of the gods, many of the stories remain the same.

SATURN: *Cronus*
God of Time and God of Sowing
Symbol: Sickle or Scythe

JUPITER: *Zeus*
King of the Gods, God of Sky, Rain, and Thunder
Symbols: Thunderbolt, Eagle, and Oak Tree

JUNO: *Hera*
Queen of the Gods, Goddess of Marriage,
  Pregnancy, and Childbirth
Symbols: Peacock, Cow, and Diadem
  (Diamond Crown)

NEPTUNE: *Poseidon*
God of the Sea
Symbols: Trident, Horse, and Dolphin

PLUTO: *Hades*
God of the Underworld
Symbols: Invisibility Helmet and Pomegranate

MINERVA: *Athena*
Goddess of Wisdom, War, and Arts and Crafts
Symbols: Owl, Shield, Loom, and Olive Tree

MARS: *Ares*
God of War
Symbols: Wild Boar, Vulture, and Dog

DIANA: *Artemis*
Goddess of the Moon and Hunt
Symbols: Deer, Moon, and Silver Bow and Arrows

APOLLO: *Apollo*
God of the Sun, Music, Healing, and Prophecy
Symbols: Laurel Tree, Lyre, Bow, and Raven

VENUS: *Aphrodite*
Goddess of Love and Beauty
Symbols: Dove, Swan, and Rose

CUPID: *Eros*
God of Love
Symbols: Bow and Arrows

MERCURY: *Hermes*
Messenger to the Gods, God of Travelers and Trade
Symbols: Crane, Caduceus, Winged Sandals,
  and Helmet

FURTHER INFORMATION

BOOKS

Namm, Diane. *Roman Myths: Retold from the Classic Originals*. New York: Sterling Publishing, 2014.

Temple, Teri. *Poseidon: God of the Sea and Earthquakes*. Mankato, MN: Child's World, 2013.

Wolfson, Evelyn. *Mythology of the Romans*. Berkeley Heights, NJ: Enslow, 2014.

WEB SITES

Visit our Web site for links about Neptune: *childsworld.com/links*

Note to Parents, Teachers, and Librarians: We routinely verify our Web links to make sure they are safe and active sites. So encourage your readers to check them out!

INDEX